Developing Reader titles are idea ⟨…⟩
using their phonics knowledge an ⟨…⟩
with only a little help. Frequently ⟨…⟩
fluency and confidence.

Special features:

.... Short, simple sentences

But the baboon was not thirsty.

Baboon was being a bully.
He stopped the other animals
from drinking from HIS waterhole.

Baboon made a big, hot fire to
scare the other animals away.

"All this water is for me!"
said Baboon. ⟨.................................. Frequent
repetition of
main story words
and phrases

6

9

Careful match
between story
and pictures

"If you want a fight, I WILL fight
you," said the little zebra.

She ran at Baboon, and up he
went over the savannah.

Large, clear ....
type

18

19

Ladybird

Educational Consultant: James Clements
Book Banding Consultant: Kate Ruttle

LADYBIRD BOOKS

UK | USA | Canada | Ireland | Australia
India | New Zealand | South Africa

Ladybird Books is part of the Penguin Random House group of companies
whose addresses can be found at global.penguinrandomhouse.com.

www.penguin.co.uk   www.puffin.co.uk   www.ladybird.co.uk

First published 2024
001

Text adapted by Abíódún Abdul
Text copyright © Ladybird Books Ltd, 2024
Illustrations by Fernando Juarez
Illustrations copyright © Ladybird Books Ltd, 2024

The moral right of the illustrator has been asserted

Printed in China

The authorized representative in the EEA is Penguin Random House Ireland,
Morrison Chambers, 32 Nassau Street, Dublin D02 YH68

A CIP catalogue record for this book is available from the British Library

ISBN: 978-0-241-56416-5

All correspondence to:
Ladybird Books
Penguin Random House Children's
One Embassy Gardens, 8 Viaduct Gardens, London SW11 7BW

MIX
Paper from
responsible sources
FSC® C018179

HOW ZEBRAS GOT THEIR STRIPES

Adapted by Abiọ́dún Abdul

Illustrated by Fernando Juarez

On the savannah, it was very hot all day. All the animals were very thirsty.

"There are not very many waterholes to drink from," said the animals.

But the baboon was not thirsty.

Baboon was being a bully.
He stopped the other animals
from drinking from HIS waterhole.

Baboon made a big, hot fire to scare the other animals away.

"All this water is for me!" said Baboon.

One day, the zebras came to drink from the waterhole.

"STOP! Go away!" shouted Baboon. He was being a bully. "This is MY waterhole!"

The big, hot fire and Baboon's shouts scared all the animals away.

But one little zebra was not scared away.

"The waterhole is for all animals!" said the little zebra.

Baboon ran at the little zebra.

"No!" shouted Baboon. "This water is all for me. Go away!"

The little zebra was not scared.

"This waterhole is for all animals," she said, again.

"There are not very many waterholes to drink from. You must let all the animals drink!"

"No!" shouted Baboon, again.
"I will not let you. Go away!
If you want to drink my water,
you must fight for it!"

"If you want a fight, I WILL fight you," said the little zebra.

She ran at Baboon, and up he went over the savannah.

His bottom came down
on to the big, hot fire.

The fire burned the hair from Baboon's bottom and made it shiny and red.

The burned sticks came down on to the zebras.

The sticks burned their hair and made stripes all over.

"I got burned!" said Baboon.

"I got burned, too!" said all
the zebras.

And this is how zebras got their stripes and how baboons got their shiny, red bottoms.

29

How much do you remember about the story of *How Zebras Got Their Stripes*? Answer these questions and find out!

- Why are the animals thirsty?

- What does Baboon make to scare the other animals away?

- Who is not scared of Baboon?

- How do the zebras get their stripes?